UNDER THE COUCH

BOOK 12

Creatures

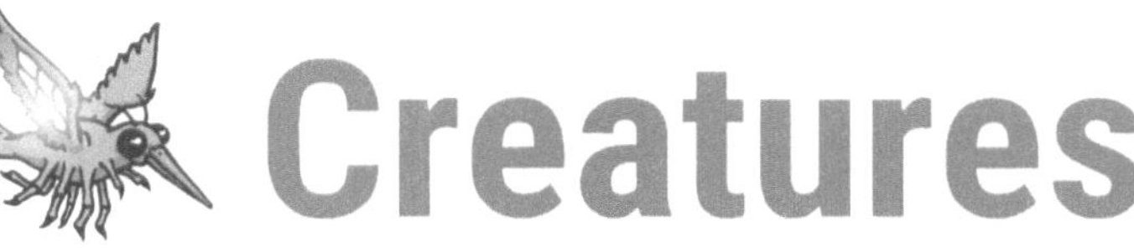

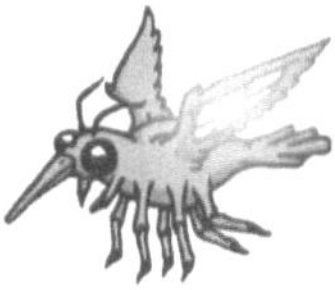

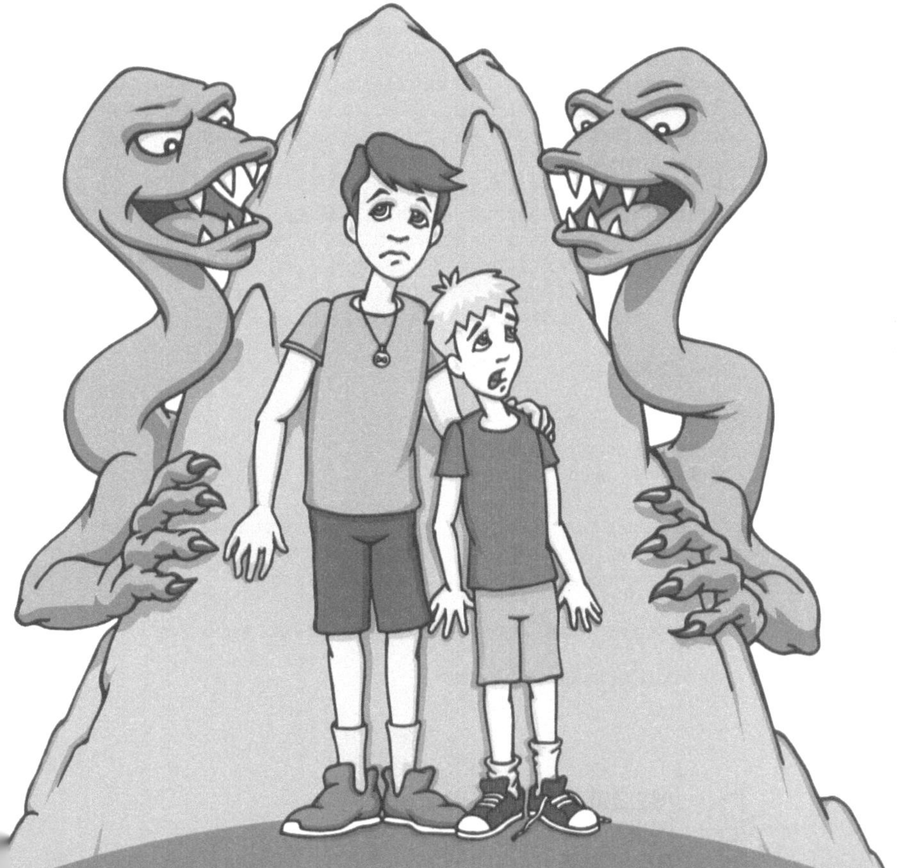

SUSAN LINTONSMITH

Creatures
Published by Passage Point Publishing, Denver, CO

Publisher's Cataloging-in-Publication data

Names: Lintonsmith, Susan, author. | Drew, Tristram, illustrator.
Title: Creatures / written by Susan Lintonsmith; illustrated by Tristram Drew.
Series: Under the Couch
Description: Denver, CO: Passage Point Publishing, 2024. | Summary: Ten-year-old Spencer and his little brother, Justin, travel to the under-the-couch world where they face scary monsters that grow larger and other strange creatures deep inside a cave!
Identifiers: ISBN: 978-1-7368911-1-7
Subjects: LCSH Monsters—Juvenile fiction. | Siblings—Juvenile fiction. | Fantasy fiction. | Adventure fiction. | BISAC JUVENILE FICTION / Fantasy & Magic | JUVENILE FICTION / Action & Adventure | JUVENILE FICTION / Readers / Intermediate | JUVENILE FICTION / Family / Siblings
Classification: LCC PZ7.1.L5645 Cre 2024 | DDC [Fic]--dc23

ISBN: 978-1-7368911-1-7

Illustrations by Tristram Drew
Cover and Interior design by Laura Drew
Editing by Shelly Wilhelm

Quantity Purchases: Schools, companies, professional groups, clubs, and other organizations may qualify for special terms when ordering quantities of this title. For information, email susan@underthecouchbooks.com.

Printed in the United States of America.

Fears are nothing more than a state of mind.
—Napoleon Hill

CONTENTS

CHAPTER
1

"I can't believe school starts next week," Spencer groaned, watching his mother pour a cup of coffee.

"Summer flew by, didn't it?" his mom replied. "I can't believe we've been in this house for three months."

Spencer looked out the kitchen window at the house next door. He remembered when the workers were digging the hole for the basement. Now the house was nearly finished. The family that bought it was moving in soon. He and Justin would finally have boys their age to play with.

"You feel any better about starting your new school?" his mother asked, sipping her coffee.

"No," he responded, nervously fiddling with the pendant around his neck that his grandma had given him for his tenth birthday. He felt anxious whenever he thought about walking into school as the new kid.

"It's nice that you've made some new friends this summer," she said.

"Yah," Spencer replied. He really liked some of the boys from his hockey clinics and was happy that a few went to his new school.

"And you'll meet even more kids you like next week," she said. "You'll have lots of new friends before you know it."

Spencer rolled his eyes. She had said that many times over the summer to make him feel better about leaving his old friends behind and moving across town at the end of the school year.

"I saw that," she said. "Seriously, this summer wasn't as bad as you thought it would be, was it?"

"Um . . . " Spencer thought about it and shook his head no.

"And it seems like you and Justin are fighting a *little* less," she noted.

"He's still annoying," Spencer mumbled. But his mom was right. He wished he could tell her all about the amazing under-the-couch adventures. The couch had changed his summer and was the reason he and his seven-year-old brother were getting along better. They spent hours at night talking about their amazing experiences that no one else knew about.

A ping coming from his mom's phone brought him out of his daze.

She read her text and then placed her coffee in the microwave to warm it. "Last week with Lori. I'm going to miss her."

"Me too," Spencer said.

"Really?" his mom asked in a high voice.

"Yah, I'm sort of sad she's leaving us," he admitted. He had grown closer to her throughout the summer, and he enjoyed their talks. Plus, he didn't know if he and Justin would be able to get through to the under-the-couch world after she left. He didn't understand why, but they could only go on adventures when she was there.

"That's a change from how you felt at the beginning of summer when you were so mad at me for hiring her," she said. "You thought she was strange."

"Oh, she's still weird," Spencer replied, thinking about his "Strange Things Lori Does" list in his journal.

"What defines normal?" his mom asked, removing her coffee from the microwave. "All I can say is that she's been an amazing help to me this summer. I couldn't have taken this new job without her. And she's offered to help out during the school year."

"Really?" Spencer smiled, brightening. *Maybe we can still go on adventures!*

They heard the garage door open, and Spencer watched Lori saunter into the kitchen.

"Good morning!" Lori sang with a huge smile on her face as she set her large shoulder bag on the counter.

"Hey," Spencer said, nodding to her. He watched her reach into her bag and pull out two bundles wrapped in tissue paper.

"Justin still sleeping?" she asked, looking around.

"Yes, he was really tired last night after your fun day," Spencer's mom replied.

They had met Spencer's new hockey friend, Drake, at the lake by Lori's house. They played catch and tag in the lake for hours. Lori was letting them choose what they wanted to do during their last week of summer.

"Good energy this morning," Lori said to Spencer after his mother left for work. "I haven't had to light candles or sage the house in a while. The spell I put on you all must be working," she said, winking.

Spencer blushed. He knew Lori was teasing him about confronting her the prior week about being a witch. He had been so convinced that he had figured out her secret. They hadn't talked about it since.

"Did you get your team assignment yet?" Lori asked.

"I made the second team," Spencer replied. He had participated in tryouts for his new hockey club over the weekend, and the night before, he had learned what team he made.

"You okay with that?" Lori asked, eyeing him. "I know you were hoping to make the top team."

"I am," Spencer responded. "Drake made the first team like I knew he would. But I'm on the same team as Jordan and Tyler who go to my new school. And Jordan only lives a few blocks away, so we can carpool to practice."

"Wonderful!" Lori said. "I'm glad you're happy."

As they talked about hockey, Justin stumbled into the kitchen, wearing his PJs.

"Good morning!" Lori said with a big smile.

"Is that a present for me?" Justin asked, pointing to the two small packages next to Lori's bag.

"One is," Lori replied, handing him the package wrapped in yellow paper. "And this is for you," she said, giving Spencer the blue bundle.

Justin tore the paper and held up two small stones. "Is this purple one the same as your ring?" he asked.

"Yes, it's amethyst — known for its ability to calm the mind and relieve stress. I knew you liked the color," Lori explained. "And the green and purple stone is green fluorite."

"It's pretty," he said, holding it close to his eye.

"It's called the student's stone. It's supposed to help with memory and be good for learning challenges like dyslexia and focus issues like ADHD," she explained.

"Did you get one for Spencer?" Justin asked. "Cuz he's got that."

"No, I don't!" Spencer shot back.

"I heard Mom and Dad say you don't focus good at school, and everyone knows your mind is always off in space," Justin said.

"No! And you shouldn't listen in on other people's conversations!" Spencer sniped, feeling his cheeks burning. "Everyone daydreams! And just because I'm more interested in some subjects and hate others doesn't mean I have ADHD!"

"Hope Ms. Lori got you a stone that helps with grumpiness," Justin muttered.

Spencer was annoyed with his brother but also knew Justin was partly right. It was hard to focus during many of his classes. But he could spend all day reading about space. He decided not to mention that because he knew Justin would tease him. "And you're the one who needs the crystal. At least I can read. You're dyslexic!" Spencer added.

"It means I'm smart and creative like

Einstein. Right, Ms. Lori?" Justin asked.

Spencer jumped in. "She said you're dyslexic like Albert Einstein, not smart like him. He could read."

"I should have looked for crystals that prevented fighting," Lori said with an exaggerated sigh. "Open your package, Spencer."

Spencer unwrapped two small crystals. "Tiger's eye," he said, smiling. He held up the light-brown polished rock with shimmers of golden yellow running through it.

"That's to replace the one you lost," she said.

Spencer had given his tiger's eye stone to a kid on one of their adventures to bribe him to keep quiet when he and Justin were trying to escape. He had told Lori he lost it, which was close to the truth.

"Tiger's eye brings strength and courage, so I wanted you to have this as you start in a new school and a new hockey team." She pointed to the smooth pink heart-shaped stone.

"And rose quartz is the stone of love. It's to remind you to be kind to yourself."

"Thanks," Spencer said, remembering that she had talked to him a lot about self-love over the summer.

"You have a necklace with that pink stone!" Justin exclaimed.

"Yes, good memory," Lori replied. "I keep in close to my heart," she said, patting her chest.

"What should I do with my crystals, Ms. Lori?" Justin asked. "Should I put them in a box like you do?"

"I'd recommend keeping the student's stone on your desk in your room for when you do homework at night . . . "

"Homework?" Justin exclaimed, throwing up his arms. "They give homework in second grade?"

Lori chuckled at Justin's theatrics. "Didn't you have homework in first grade?" she asked.

"No!" Justin insisted.

"Your homework is probably still scrunched

up at the bottom of your backpack," Spencer said with a smirk, knowing that Justin's school bag was always a mess.

Lori stepped between them. "The good news is that you don't have to worry about school until next week. Let's focus on the present and head to the park by the pool. Then we can swim for a bit after that. I'll pack a picnic while you two get ready."

The boys raced upstairs to get their swimsuits.

CHAPTER 2

After a full day at the park and the pool, they got home in time for Lori's TV show.

"What are you planning to do when we go back to school?" Spencer asked as he watched Lori make tea. He was happy that she planned to watch her program so he and Justin could go on an adventure. He didn't know if they'd have another chance.

"I'm teaching kindergarten again this year," Lori responded. "I go back to school next week as well."

"Do you like working with little kids? I mean, aren't they annoying?" Spencer asked, nodding his head toward Justin.

"I love kids," she responded, grabbing a yellow tea container from her oversized bag.

"What's that?" Spencer asked, motioning to the box.

"It's called Native American Good Medicine." She read from the side of the box: "American Indians believe that Mother Earth has provided us with plants and herbs that are essential in maintaining good health."

Spencer nodded. He remembered that Lori's great-great-grandma, Luyu, was Indigenous.

"Smells minty," he said, sniffing the air.

"It's a blend of spearmint, eucalyptus, and other natural herbs," Lori said, looking at the ingredients on the box. "It's supposed to lift your spirits and put you in a good mood."

"You need to give that to Spencer," Justin blurted from his seat at the kitchen table, where he had dumped a pile of Legos. "You know, cuz he's always grumpy?"

"You're the one who puts me in a bad mood!" Spencer growled.

"Could use it, just saying," Justin said under his breath, connecting two Legos.

Lori stifled a laugh. "You sure you don't mind if I watch my show today?" she asked. "I can skip it since we only have a few days left together."

"No, you should watch it," Spencer quickly responded, glancing at the clock. Her show was starting in a few minutes.

"Then let's skip reading and play video games after my program," Lori suggested as she headed to the family room.

"Yes! That's an even better gift than the crystals!" Justin cheered, making Lori chuckle.

Once Lori was absorbed in her TV show, Spencer and Justin crept into the living room and stood in front of the cream-colored couch that their dad had purchased at an antique store in the mountains.

"I've been looking forward to this all week!" Justin said, getting down on the floor to crawl under the couch.

"Me too," Spencer said, glancing back at the family room. He could see Lori's short black hair sticking up over the back of her chair. He always worried that Lori would look for them while they were on their adventures. So far, she hadn't noticed when they were gone. Fortunately, hours in the under-the-couch world were only minutes at home.

Spencer lay on the floor and lifted the couch skirt. In the dim light, he could see Justin leaning against the back wall with a big grin on his face. Then his brother disappeared.

Spencer blinked, staring at the empty spot. After going on adventures all summer, he still had no idea how they got through.

He slid under and took Justin's place against the wall, feeling around the floor. As usual, everything was normal.

His stomach fluttered as he leaned against the wall and waited. He loved going under the couch but always worried about possible dangers and whether they'd get back safely.

Suddenly, Spencer dropped into the dark abyss. He screamed and flailed his arms around until he felt the steel slide under him.

He slid straight down and then back up as the slide curved in a "U." He flew off the edge at the top. Again, he screamed as he floundered in midair. The slide caught him. He sped down and back up before flying off the edge again. This happened three more times before he stayed on the slide and sped around in tight circles. He shot off the bottom and landed hard on the padded floor in the hallway.

"You still land on your butt after all these times," Justin said, giggling. "What was up with all the screaming?"

"The slide kept tossing me off!" Spencer said. "It was crazy."

"The slide spun me around so many times I'm still dizzy," Justin said, turning in circles to demonstrate.

Spencer got to his feet and followed Justin down the hall toward the large black door. He kept an eye on the wall to his left. The strange flame-like lights flickered brightly in the mirrored wall, as if saying hello. But surprisingly, the woman in black wasn't there.

"Are you hearing me?" Justin asked, annoyed.

Where is she today? Spencer wondered. He stopped and leaned closer to the wall.

"Lori should have given you that rock that helps you pay attention," Justin said.

"Yah," Spencer responded absentmindedly, remembering how frightened he used to be by the strange old woman. Now he actually *wanted* to see her. He was less afraid and wanted to understand who or what she was. He didn't know why she was in the under-the-couch world.

"You know I can't open this door by myself," Justin said. "Hello?"

"Oh," Spencer replied, backing away from the wall. He joined his brother in front of the massive door, glancing back at the still-empty wall.

Spencer placed his hand on the metal handle next to Justin's. The door opened, letting them into the circular room. As it shut behind them, Spencer looked around the big room and saw the hundreds of unique doors covering the walls.

"Dark in here today," Justin noted.

Spencer scanned across the high domed ceiling at the four C-shaped moons that stood out among the thousands of stars.

"Waning crescent moons. Next time we come, they'll be new moons." *If there is a next time.*

"You can't see a new moon, so it'll be really dark," Justin said, passing by the giant marble in the middle of the room.

"Wow, you actually learned something

about the phases of the moon this summer," Spencer said sarcastically.

"I tried not to, but you talked about it so much that it got stuck in my brain," Justin replied.

Spencer smirked at his brother's response. After gazing up at the stars and moons, he headed over to the glowing blue marble. He could hear Justin talking, but he was distracted by the wispy white forms that were swirling around on the surface of the stone. As he approached, the forms floated away in different directions, leaving a deep blue circle.

Spencer hesitated. He knew from past adventures the strange effect the marble had on him. "I won't let it happen today. I'll just quickly see what the stone is showing me," he whispered, looking into the blue surface.

He grew dizzy as the beautiful blue faded to white. Suddenly, he was standing in front of a whiteboard. Confused, he turned around and was surprised to see that he was at the front of a classroom. Kids his age poured into the room. Spencer studied the faces but didn't recognize anyone.

A girl with big brown eyes and long brown hair approached him. "You must be the new kid," she said. "I'm Jillian. What's your name?"

Spencer opened his mouth, but no words came out. *What's happening? Why can't I speak?* He pushed from his belly to say his name. *Spencer! I'm Spencer,* he said in his head. But all he heard was an awkward grunt, and he turned red with embarrassment.

Jillian gave him a strange look and walked away.

CHAPTER
3

What's the matter with me? Spencer wondered, feeling sweaty. *I'm such an idiot!* He couldn't believe he had just grunted at the nice girl.

He looked around the classroom. The desks were filling up. A teacher with long dark hair and green eyes came over.

"You can sit here," she said, pointing to an empty desk.

Spencer sat down and rested his head in his hands. He wanted to disappear.

"Hey new kid, you okay?" a red-haired girl asked.

He looked at the girl and tried to respond, but again, no words came out. He turned back and stared blankly at the whiteboard.

A bell rang. The teacher closed the door and walked to the front of the room.

"Class, we have a new student I'd like you to meet," she said.

No, please don't focus on me! Spencer screamed in his head.

"Spencer, can you come up here, please?" the teacher asked, smiling.

Spencer forced himself to walk to the front of the class. His legs felt like noodles as the eyes of thirty kids studied him. He glanced quickly at the door, thinking about bolting out of the room.

Then something landed in his hair. He brushed it off and watched a large blue feather float to the ground. He looked up and saw his classmates staring at him. The snickers made him feel like he had been punched in the gut.

"Spencer?" the teacher repeated, trying to fill the awkward silence. "Please tell us about yourself. Where did you live before this? What are your hobbies?"

Spencer again tried to speak and instead made a croaking sound. It was like a giant pancake was stuck in his vocal cords. He cringed and twisted his hands together as he heard more sneers.

Another feather landed on his head. He looked up, shocked to see hundreds of bright blue feathers floating down from the ceiling. They blocked his view so he couldn't see the class.

Then, magically, he could talk. The words flowed easily. He told everyone about himself.

After he finished talking, the blue feathers stopped falling. He could see his classmates again. Some kids were smiling but not in a mocking way. He started to brush the feathers off his shirt but they were gone. He looked around at the floor. Nothing.

"Where did the feathers go?" Spencer asked.

"What feathers?" someone asked.

"The blue feathers," Spencer said. "There were so many that I couldn't even see you."

"Are you even awake?" a kid asked.

Spencer blinked and stared into Justin's face. He looked around and realized he was back in the circular room, standing in front of the marble.

"You never learn," Justin said, shaking his head. "You let it happen again."

Spencer rubbed his temples. "It seemed so real."

"Cuz it's a giant moonrock and Ms. Lori said they can make you dream," Justin replied.

"Moonstone," Spencer corrected. He had written about his dreams in the second section of his journal. He had figured out that each experience had a meaning. He assumed this dream was because he was anxious about school starting. *No way could my first day be that bad!* He made a mental note to look up the meaning of a blue feather.

"Come see the door I picked," Justin said, heading over to a giant gray rock covered with orange glowing lights.

"Creepy," Spencer said. "The lights look like a bunch of eyes staring at us."

"I like it," Justin retorted. "It's different from the other doors we've picked, and you know I always choose the best adventures."

"Whatever," Spencer mumbled. His brother wouldn't let him forget the time he selected a door that took them to a farm filled with vegetable gardens and a barn full of spiders.

"Help me open it," Justin said.

They knew from past adventures that they had to touch the same spot on the door to make it open. They pressed on different areas and tried pushing on the door, but nothing happened. They tapped nearly every orange circle. Finally, they touched a circle toward the bottom, and all the circles started flashing.

The huge rock rolled forward a few feet, leaving a hole in the wall.

Spencer followed Justin through the opening and around the boulder. Beyond it, the sky was gray and it smelled like rain. The ground was still damp. Spencer watched the huge rock roll back against the hill, blocking the entrance to the circular room.

"I've never seen so many big rocks!" Justin exclaimed.

"It's going to be hard to find our door," Spencer pointed out. "We'll have to mark it well." He collected sticks and made an arrow pointing to the boulder. Then they gathered several grapefruit-sized rocks and lined them up before the arrow. Spencer looked up the hill and noted the blue and green wildflowers above where their door had been.

"Okay, I think we're good," Spencer said. "Let's take that path over there."

They hiked up a muddy trail through a field of wildflowers and tall grasses.

"I wonder what's going to happen on

this adventure," Justin said. "There's nothing around here but rocks. Hope we find something fun to do."

"I don't see anything interesting this way. Let's go another way," Spencer suggested.

They had walked for a minute when suddenly, Spencer froze. "I heard something," he whispered.

"I didn't hear anything," Justin said.

"Shhhh," Spencer said, listening. He studied the wildflowers to his right that were swaying gently in the light breeze. "Something's in the field."

"I hear it," Justin whispered. "Maybe an animal?"

Suddenly, a spiky blue-green head the size of a softball popped up from the tall weeds. It opened its mouth and growled, revealing sharp teeth.

"Ahhhh!" Spencer yelled, stepping back and nearly tripping over his brother.

The creature got taller, and its head grew to the size of a basketball. Heads of different sizes and colors started popping up all over the field.

"Monsters!" Justin shrieked.

An orange creature with horns on top of its head shot up above the wild grass. A yellow figure doubled in size and turned its head so its five eyes could study the boys.

"Why are they getting bigger?" Justin yelled, stepping behind Spencer as a red creature with seven arms grew another two feet.

"We have to get out of here!" Spencer yelled. He looked in the direction of their door and saw big, scary creatures lumbering toward them. "This way!" he shouted, grabbing Justin's arm and pulling him in the opposite direction. They ran down the hill and across the field.

Justin turned to look at the creatures following behind. "There's more of them! And they're still growing!"

"Follow me!" Spencer hollered. They ran as fast as they could to the rocky hill. They slid behind a large boulder and crouched down to catch their breath.

"That was scary!" Justin whispered. "Do you think we lost them?"

Spencer looked up and saw a gray head with three green eyes staring down at them. "Nope!"

CHAPTER
4

"Go away monster!" Justin shouted.

The creature grew bigger. Its head doubled in size and got stuck between the boulder and the side of the hill.

That gave Spencer a few seconds to look out from behind the rock.

"I see a small opening in the hill over there," he told Justin. "Run, and don't slow down until we're inside!"

They raced through the field and around rocks and trees to the opening. They flew inside the cave and pressed themselves against the wall in the shadows.

"They're too big to get in here, right?" Justin asked, breathing heavily.

"Yah, but they can grow, so maybe they can also shrink," Spencer said. He looked around the inside of the cave. "I really don't want to go any farther than this. Who knows what creepy creatures live in here."

Suddenly, the cave grew darker as a brown monster with yellow spots blocked the entrance.

"Arggh!" Justin screamed, running away from the opening and toward the back of the cave. "Where do we go?"

"Head for the smallest opening!" Spencer shouted, running after his brother. They ducked into a narrow passageway and crouched down.

"I don't like it in this cave," Justin complained. "It's too dark, and I'm cold!"

"Hopefully, the monsters will go away and we can go back outside," Spencer whispered.

Justin stared past Spencer. He clutched his brother's arm. "What . . . what are those?"

Spencer looked where Justin was pointing. It took his eyes a second to adjust to the darkness. Then he saw them. Small black figures were hanging upside down along the ceiling. Dozens of glowing orange eyes stared at them.

Spencer cursed. "We have to get out of here . . . "

"What are they?" Justin asked, shaking from fright and cold.

"Bats," Spencer replied.

"WHAT?" Justin screamed. He stood up and bolted out of their hiding place.

The startled bats flew off their perches and toward Spencer. He shrieked as the flapping wings brushed against him. He covered his head with his arms and ran out behind Justin.

"Why'd you do that?!" Spencer yelled as he made his way to the mouth of the cave. He grabbed his screaming brother and pulled him against the wall to avoid the stream of bats that circled in a fury around them. Finally, one flew out of the cave entrance, and the others followed.

"Those were awful!" Justin yelped after the last one left.

"You shouldn't have screamed like that! You disturbed them, and they flew right at my face!" Spencer scolded, struggling to stand on his jiggly legs.

"I couldn't help it! They scared me," Justin cried. "I want out of here!"

"Wait!" Spencer said, pulling Justin back. "Let me see if the coast is clear." Spencer poked his head out of the cave entrance and quickly jerked back. "The monsters are still out there. We have to stay here longer."

"No, I don't want to!" Justin whined.

Suddenly, the brown monster stepped into the cave. This time, it was half the size it was before.

"How'd it get smaller?" Justin screamed.

Immediately, the monster grew bigger until it completely blocked the opening to the cave.

"Head to a tunnel!" Spencer shouted, pulling his brother by the shirt.

"No, there are bats in there!" Justin screamed.

Spencer frantically looked around and spotted a different tunnel. "That one!"

He held his breath as they entered. Spencer didn't know if he was more afraid of the monster behind them or what they might find in the dark lair ahead.

As they hurried down the path, Spencer kept an eye on the ceiling for bats.

"I can't see where I'm going," Justin grumbled.

Spencer slowed his pace. Sweat dripped down his face, despite the cold.

They continued slowly through the tunnel until it opened into a big chamber. Faint light poked in through cracks in the rocks.

"Oh, thank you," Spencer said, exhaling a sigh of relief.

"This place looks like a monster's mouth," Justin said, rubbing the goosebumps on his arms. "Don't those rocks look like sharp, pointy teeth coming from the ceiling and floor?"

"Stalactites and stalagmites," Spencer said, staring at the icicle-looking rock formations. "Dad taught us that when we toured the cave last summer. He said stalactites are the ones that hang from the ceiling because they have to hold on *tight*." He motioned to the ground. "And don't step on the stalagmites because it *might* hurt. So, be careful where you step."

"I already stepped in something wet," Justin said, looking down at the small puddle he was standing in.

"Probably from the rain," Spencer said, glancing around the ceiling of the cave. "And there's light coming through. Maybe there's an opening. If we can find another way out, then we don't have to go back out where the bats and monsters are."

"I don't want to ever see them again," Justin said, shaking his head.

"I'll go this way to look for a way out. You go that way," Spencer instructed.

Spencer slowly navigated around the sharp rocks, searching the cave for openings. He spotted water dripping down the side of the cave wall. He climbed up a pile of rocks to see where it was coming from. Light streamed in from a small opening, but it was too small to fit through. He pushed on the rock to see if he could make the hole bigger, but it wouldn't budge.

Suddenly, a scream pierced the silence.

"HELP!" Justin yelled from far away.

"What happened? Are you okay?" Spencer shouted, climbing quickly down the rockpile and returning to where he had left his brother. "Where are you?"

"Down here!" Justin cried. "I fell!"

Spencer saw a hole in the floor. He poked his head through and could barely see his brother far below.

"Are you okay?" Spencer asked again, feeling sick to his stomach. *No, he's not! He just fell about forty feet and landed on rocks!*

"Something's wrong!" Justin yelled. "I can't move!"

No! Did he break his back? "Hold on, I'm coming!" Spencer responded.

He cringed, thinking about Justin's body landing on the sharp rocks. *Why didn't I stay next to him?* Knowing he had to get to him fast, Spencer thought about dropping through the hole. But it was a long way and he couldn't risk getting hurt, too.

Spencer looked around at the different paths and selected one. As he walked through the dimly lit space, he sensed it was taking him in the wrong direction. He went back and chose another path, but it was a dead end. He had only gotten about twenty feet into the next tunnel when he felt sticky threads hit his face.

"No! No! No!" he yelled, furiously brushing cobwebs out of his hair. "I hate spiders!"

He ran back to the entrance of the tunnel. He chose the last passageway and tentatively walked into the opening, watching the ceiling for cobwebs and bats.

"Hang on, I'm coming!" Spencer called out, hoping Justin could hear him. He carefully hiked down the steep and rocky path to get to his injured brother. *What if Justin can't walk? How am I going to carry him back up this hill?*

Spencer breathed a sigh of relief as the trail wrapped around and led him into the room where Justin had fallen.

"I'm here," Spencer said softly.

"Help me! I can't move!" Justin cried.

CHAPTER 5

Spencer could barely see across the room. Faint light was coming through an opening in the wall on the other side, which helped him see the sharp rocks that covered the floor. Spencer braced himself for seeing his brother's broken little body.

"Can you feel anything?" Spencer asked.

"It's so sticky!" Justin replied.

He must be covered in blood. Spencer navigated around the rocks and was finally close enough to see his brother. "What the . . ." It took him a few seconds to process what he was seeing.

"Get me out of this!" Justin yelled, trying to move. "I'm stuck!"

Instead of lying on the sharp rocks, as Spencer imagined, Justin was floating horizontally about four feet above the ground!

"You didn't land on the rocks?" Spencer asked. "You're not hurt?"

"I hate this! Help me!" Justin shouted. He was stuck like a human fly in a giant spiderweb.

"I can't believe you didn't hit the ground . . ." Spencer started. Then the relief faded as he saw the size of the web that stretched across the room and entangled his brother. Chills ran down his spine as he imagined what could have made a web big and strong enough to stop a falling boy in midair.

Spencer jerked his head around. The dim light coming out of the wall wasn't enough to see all corners of the dark room. He felt weak with fright and took a few deep breaths to calm down.

"We need to get out of here," Spencer whispered, pulling on Justin's arm. His brother barely moved in the sticky net. "Ugh, it's like you're glued down!"

"I want out!" Justin whined.

Spencer rubbed his sticky hands on his shorts, but the goo wouldn't come off.

"I don't want to get stuck in the web with you," Spencer said. "Let me find something to cut it." He picked up a sharp rock and used the edges to slice at the web around Justin's legs.

"Try to stand," he instructed once Justin's legs were freed.

Justin hung vertically in the air about two feet from the ground, but his upper body was still wrapped firmly in the web. Spencer grabbed a clean stone and continued to chop at the web.

Finally, Justin was free from his trap and able to stand on the ground.

"I can't get this sticky stuff off of me!" Justin cried as he furiously rubbed his head and face.

Spencer tried to help. "I'm covered in it, too. I don't think it's coming off," he said. "Let's get out of here and find a place to wash off."

As they turned to head back to the passageway, Justin froze.

"What was that?" he asked, referring to the sound of clattering feet across the rocks.

Spencer shook with fear as something big and black moved from the shadows. Both boys shrieked in terror as an eight-legged creature that looked the size of a Volkswagen Bug blocked the opening of the tunnel.

Spencer cursed and frantically searched for an escape route.

"What do we do?" Justin cried, backing away from the giant spider.

Spencer pointed at the small hole in the wall where faint light was coming through. "Go through that opening!"

Justin didn't hesitate. He bolted around the sharp rocks and quickly flew through the wall.

When the enormous black creature moved one of its legs, Spencer let out a piercing scream and sprinted after Justin, nearly tripping over rocks in his path.

"Help me!" Spencer yelled as he dove headfirst through the opening that was only a little over a foot wide.

Justin pulled Spencer through the wall and into a different room of the cave. Spencer landed on the ground with a thud. He quickly crawled away from the hole and struggled to his feet.

"Think it can get through?" Justin asked, running past Spencer down the path.

"I hope not!" Spencer shouted, racing to catch up with his brother.

They sprinted down the hill into the cavern below. Finally, they stopped and looked back at the wall. The giant spider had one leg through the hole but wasn't able to fit its large body through the opening.

"There better not be any more of those horrible spiders in here!" Justin said in a shaky voice. "That was awful — worse than the monsters outside!"

"I could puke," Spencer said, still watching the wall. Reassured that the spider wasn't getting through, he lifted his sticky shirt to examine the scrapes on his stomach from being pulled through the opening. His skin was red and irritated, but he wasn't bleeding. He rubbed his hands together. "We need to get this stuff off."

"I think there's water down there," Justin said, pointing down the rocky slope to the other side of the cavern.

Spencer sighed with relief at the sight of glimmering water. "Let's go!"

"Why is it glowing?" Justin asked as they hiked toward the water.

"I don't know," Spencer said, looking around. He had been so freaked out by the giant spider that he hadn't thought about why it was lighter in this section of the cave.

Justin pointed to the ceiling. "From those flying bugs?"

Bird-sized creatures circled the top of the cave, and their foot-long wings glowed as they rapidly moved up and down.

"What are they?" Spencer wondered aloud.

"I hear humming. Think they're giant hummingbirds?" Justin asked.

"They look a little like lightning bugs," Spencer said.

"So, they're bird-bugs."

"Good one," Spencer said, smiling despite his nerves.

"How are they making that sound?" Justin asked.

Spencer studied the strange creatures. "I think it's coming from their wings."

"Like crickets," Justin stated.

"No, crickets make noise rubbing their legs together," Spencer said.

"Dad told me they sing with their wings," Justin corrected. "I remembered cuz it rhymes. And he said that hummingbirds make sounds with their feathers." Justin grinned, proud of himself.

"I didn't know crickets had wings," Spencer muttered, watching the creatures. "Looks like they're eating something off the ceiling, so hopefully they won't want to eat us. Let's hurry and get washed up and get out of here."

Justin hummed along with the tune as they approached the pond.

"Gross! It smells like rotten eggs!" Justin complained. "Think it's safe to go in?" he asked, dunking his hands in the stinky water to rub the sticky goo off.

"Smells like sulfur — like the well water at Grandpa and Grandma's house," Spencer replied. "And fortunately for you, since you're already in the water, it should be fine." Spencer joined his brother to wash off.

"It stinks, but at least it's warm," Justin said, scrubbing his hair to get the webs out.

When they were clean and no longer sticky, they climbed out and sat on a large rock to dry off. Spencer's stomach started to hurt as he thought about being lost deep in the cave with strange creatures all around.

"We need to figure out another way out of here," he said. "We obviously can't go back where that horrible spider is."

Not hearing a response, he looked over at Justin, who was grinning as he stared into the water. He was slowly rocking and humming along with the sound from the glowing bird-bugs.

"You don't seem very concerned," Spencer grunted. "Am I the only one worried about how we're getting out of here?"

"Just relaxing," Justin replied, yawning. He returned to humming.

Spencer frowned. As usual, it was up to him to get them out of this mess. He closed his eyes, trying to focus on what they should do. But he couldn't think. He was too distracted by the humming. He wanted to yell at his brother.

Next thing he knew, he was falling forward.

CHAPTER
6

Spencer woke up as he landed in the water.

Shocked, he quickly moved to the side of the pond and got out.

"What was that?" Justin asked once he finished laughing. "I thought we were drying off?"

"I think I fell asleep!" Spencer exclaimed.

"I could fall asleep right now," Justin said. "I'm so tired."

"No, you don't understand! I was panicking about how we're going to get out of here, and next thing I know, I'm waking up in the water!" Spencer replied.

"Yah, really strange," Justin said, giggling. Then he yawned again.

Spencer shook his head to clear it. "We can't fall asleep. We need to get out of here."

"Think there's another way out?" Justin asked groggily.

"There has to be. This cave is huge," Spencer replied. "Let's start walking . . . that way."

They hiked away from the water and the bird-bugs and deeper into the cavern. Soon the cave grew darker.

"Brrr, it's even colder when you're wet," Justin said, shivering.

They moved around a wall formed by stalagmites and into a brighter room filled with what looked like huge, clear forms.

"Is that ice?" Justin asked.

"Looks like it," Spencer said, gliding his

hand across the smooth surface. "But it's not cold. I think it's crystals."

"I like it in here," Justin said, smiling. "I'm not as tired."

"I feel a little lightheaded," Spencer replied, sitting down on one of the stone structures. Soon, his stomach stopped hurting and he smiled. "I feel better in here. Think it could have something to do with the crystals?"

"Ms. Lori says some of hers make her feel happier," Justin said.

Spencer felt a pang in his stomach as he thought about his nanny and being so far from home. Then, as he leaned against the wall of crystals, his mind relaxed, and he felt calm again.

Justin started giggling as he laid back on a large crystal.

"What's so funny?" Spencer asked, looking at him strangely.

"I don't know," Justin answered. "I was thinking about the monsters, the bats, the giant spider . . . you face-planting in the water . . . "

He couldn't finish; he was laughing so hard. Spencer couldn't help but chuckle with his brother.

Finally, Justin stopped and wiped the tears from his eyes.

"I wonder what type of crystal this is," Spencer said, picking a small stone off the ground that looked like a rectangular ice cube. Holding it made him feel optimistic. "We're going to be okay. We'll find a way out," Spencer said, trying to reassure his brother. "But we should get going."

They left the crystal room and continued walking through the cave.

"Hey, a butterfly!" Justin exclaimed. A brown and yellow butterfly flew right in front of them and down the path as if leading the way.

They followed the butterfly through the cave and into a section where sunlight peeked through cracks in rocks. The butterfly flew up toward the light.

"I think there's an opening up there!" Spencer exclaimed, pointing to where the butterfly was heading.

The boys climbed the rocks. As they got closer, the light grew bigger.

"Yes!" Justin shouted when they got to an opening large enough for them to climb through.

They shielded their eyes as they stepped out into the sunlight.

"We did it!" Justin shouted again, giving Spencer a high five.

"I'm so glad to be outside," Spencer said, smiling. "Not gonna lie . . . being lost in the cave freaked me out."

Justin nodded in agreement. Then he looked around. "Which way is our door?" he asked.

"Let me think," Spencer said, trying to retrace in his head their path through the enormous cave. "I think we entered the cave over there," he said, motioning to the other side of the hill. "We're lower than where we came in, so first we have to go up."

They hiked to the top of the hill and then took a narrow path that eventually led them to a field of long grasses and wildflowers.

"Is this the same field we saw before?" Justin asked.

"I was wondering the same thing," Spencer replied. "If it is, then our door should be that way."

As they headed toward their door, Justin kept an eye on the long wildflowers and grasses that waved gently with the breeze. "I think this is where we saw the scary monsters," he said.

"Let's keep quiet just in case," Spencer suggested.

Justin gasped and grabbed his brother's arm. "I heard something," he said, staring at the wildflowers. Just then, colorful heads started popping up over the tall grass.

"No, not again!" Spencer groaned. "Run for the door!"

They started down the path but were stopped in their tracks by a bright blue monster with white stripes.

"Other way!" Spencer yelled, grabbing his brother's arm. They ran to a group of large boulders.

"Hide behind them?" Justin yelled.

"No, go up!" Spencer shouted, glancing back at the creatures. "They're getting bigger, so we have to go higher!" Spencer boosted Justin on top of the rock and then climbed up behind him. "Keep going!" he yelled, pushing his little brother up the next rock.

A green two-headed creature approached the rock and swung one of its large heads toward Spencer's leg.

"Get away!" Justin shouted, kicking at it so Spencer could finish climbing up the second rock.

A purple creature with white polka dots moved beside the green one. It stretched its long neck and sniffed the boys. The green monster growled, showing two rows of sharp teeth.

Justin screamed.

Both creatures grew another foot. They were now taller than the rocks the boys were standing on.

Spencer cried out as both of the green heads snapped at his legs. He looked behind him and saw that the next rock was too big to climb. They wouldn't be able to go higher.

More monsters arrived and surrounded the rock. The boys continued to swat the heads away, but there were too many creatures to fight off.

The boys were trapped.

They both screamed.

CHAPTER
7

"Stop!" a voice hollered from above them on the hill. "You have to stop being afraid!"

"Help us!" Spencer yelled, feeling a little relieved someone was there.

"They're going to eat us!" Justin added.

"Laugh!" a girl instructed.

"What?!" Spencer shouted. "We're about to be dinner!"

"Do it now!" she yelled. "Laugh!"

Spencer grunted as he pulled Justin away from the purple monster.

"Do you think that one farts purple air?" a boy's voice asked.

Despite his fear, Justin giggled.

"I bet his farts smell like grapes," the boy added, making Justin chuckle again.

"That kid has your sense of humor," Spencer said, pulling Justin away to avoid another snap from a green head.

"What should you say when you meet a two-headed monster?" the boy asked. "Goodbye, goodbye!" he answered. "Get it? Because the green one has two heads?"

Justin laughed louder.

"Hey, I think they just got smaller!" Spencer exclaimed, shocked to see the monsters shrink a foot.

"You can't show fear," the girl yelled. "That makes them bigger!"

Spencer wouldn't have believed the strange girl if he hadn't seen the monsters get smaller when they laughed.

"What does a monster drive?" Justin called over his shoulder as he jerked out of the path of a long, spotted arm reaching toward him.

"A monster truck!" the boy on the hill responded.

Justin cracked up at his own joke. The creatures shrank again, no longer able to reach the boys.

"Why did the vampire go into the cave?" the boy asked. "To hang out."

"I think we just saw him," Justin said, snorting.

Spencer cracked up. The creatures shrunk to the size of a horse.

"Okay, enough with the horrible jokes!" Spencer said.

The boy and girl behind them chuckled. The laughter was contagious, and soon all four of them were howling. The creatures shrank to the size of cats and ran back to the long grasses.

Once Spencer was sure the creatures were gone, he helped Justin down from the rocks.

The boy and girl hiked down the hill and joined them.

"Glad you guys were here," Justin said. "We were almost monster snacks!"

"Glad you listened to me and laughed," the girl replied. "Your fear of them made them grow bigger."

Spencer stared at the girl. She was around his age and had short dark hair and glasses. Next to her was a younger boy with dark hair. He was about two inches shorter.

"I know you!" Spencer shouted. "I can't believe it! How is it possible you are here?"

"Have we met?" the girl asked, looking at him strangely. "I don't think I know you."

Spencer's mouth hung open in disbelief. "I don't understand how this is happening!" He knew them! He had seen them in a picture. And the girl had been in one of his dreams in the giant marble.

Justin stepped forward. "I'm Justin, and this is my brother, Spencer."

"Nice to meet you," the girl said. "I'm . . . "

"You're Lori!" Spencer blurted out.

"How do you know my name?" she asked, shocked.

"And you're Leo!" Spencer yelled, pointing to the boy.

"Yah," the boy responded. "Sorry dude, but I don't know you."

"We've never met," Spencer said to Leo. "But I've heard a lot about you."

"Hold on a minute!" Justin shouted, waving his arms. "Are you telling me that girl is Lori . . . as in Ms. Lori?"

"Okay, you guys are freaking me out," the girl said, backing up. "What is going on here?"

"I don't know how to explain . . . " Spencer started.

"Ms. Lori? Our nanny?" Justin asked again in a higher voice.

"Look, I'm only ten. I don't even babysit yet. You have the wrong person. We're not from anywhere around here," she said, obviously shaken. She grabbed Leo's arm to pull him away.

"Yah, we're just visiting," Leo added while being dragged by his sister.

"I can't believe it!" Spencer exclaimed. "I had no idea you went on adventures, too!"

The two kids stopped and looked back at him.

"Too? You mean, you're not from here?" Lori asked, looking confused. "You're on an adventure?"

"Yes," Spencer answered. "We're from Colorado, same as you."

Lori and Leo looked stunned.

"We've never run into anyone else who was on an adventure," Leo said. "And no one has ever known our names or where we're from."

"What else do you know about us?" Lori asked, challenging Spencer.

"I know you're close to your grandma," Spencer replied. Ms. Lori had told him about how she loved spending time with her grandmother in the mountains.

"Lots of kids are," Lori said, visibly shaken.

"But you're extra close to your Grandma

Laurel. And she was close to her grandmother, the one who came from the Ute Tribe."

"Okay, WHAT'S GOING ON?" she shouted. "Who are you? And why do you know so much about us?"

"Yah, dude. Really strange," Leo added.

"I'm not sure I understand it either," Spencer said, his mind racing.

"Do you go under a couch to go on your adventure?" Justin asked.

"How . . . how do you know about that?" Leo stuttered.

"Okay, seriously, how did you get that information?" the girl demanded. "Are you mind readers or something?"

"No, but do you go under a couch?" Spencer asked again. *Is it possible that there are two magical couches?*

Lori and Leo glanced at each other. Finally, Lori sighed and nodded. "Yes, at my grandmother's house."

"We go under a cream couch at our new house," Justin said.

Young Lori sat down on a rock, trying to process what she was hearing. "I just assumed my grandmother's couch was one of a kind. I can't believe there's another one like it."

Spencer's head was spinning as he started to put the puzzle pieces together. His dad found their couch at an antique store in the mountains. It used to belong to an old woman. He knew the couch was at least two hundred years old. *Was it possible?*

"Maybe there's only one couch," Spencer whispered.

"No, that makes no sense. My grandma's couch is red, and it's at her house. Your brother said your couch is cream and at your new house," Leo pointed out.

Spencer knew that their couch was old but had newer fabric on it. *Was it red before that?*

"Okay, so we both have a magical couch and go on adventures," Lori stated. "I still don't understand how you know our names or where we're from."

"It's complicated," Spencer responded, not sure how to explain that they were from her future when she is their nanny and in her forties.

He felt uncomfortable under Lori's stare. Her big brown eyes looked bigger through her glasses. It reminded him of Ms. Lori doing the same thing when she knew he was keeping something from her.

Lori glanced at her watch. "Leo, we need to go."

"Already?" Justin whined. "Why?"

"We need to get back before our grandma notices we're gone," she replied.

"But time is different on adventures. Hours here are like minutes at home," Spencer said, hoping she'd stay longer. He had so much to talk to her about.

"I know. But there's a limit to how long you can stay," Lori said.

"Maybe you can help us find our door home," Leo said. "We were looking for it when we heard you screaming."

"We'd be happy to help," Spencer offered.

"No, we're fine," Lori replied. "We can find it on our own."

"But, Lori, we've been looking for a long time and haven't been able to," Leo retorted.

"We don't need their help!" Lori barked.

Spencer stared at the stubborn girl. He still couldn't believe this was his nanny.

"Has it ever happened before . . . where you can't find the door back?" Spencer asked.

Lori looked annoyed but thought about his question. "Never," she finally replied.

"Sometimes we don't find our door until we learn something," Spencer said, trying to be helpful.

"I think it's because two strange boys distracted us, and we aren't looking for it. Come on, Leo, let's retrace our steps again. Goodbye." Lori turned and headed up the hill.

"Bye, nice to meet you," Leo said as he reluctantly followed her.

CHAPTER
8

"I can't believe that's Ms. Lori," Justin said, watching them leave. "I like the old Ms. Lori better. She's nicer."

"Yah, young Lori is stubborn and doesn't want anyone to help her." Spencer turned to face the long grasses and wildflowers. "We should probably get back to our door."

They hadn't gone far when they heard a scream.

Spencer and Justin raced back to find a very upset Lori.

"It took him!" Lori cried. "It's got Leo!"

"What took him?" Spencer asked, looking around but seeing no one.

"A . . . a strange creature!" she stammered. "I was looking for our door and heard something behind me. I turned and there it was! It grabbed Leo and ran in that direction. We have to hurry!"

"Okay, we're going to help. I promise, we'll get him back," Spencer said, trying to settle her down.

"Was it one of the monsters?" Justin asked.

"No, it was different. I've never seen anything like it! It stood on two feet and looked sort of like a . . . a cross between an animal and a giant troll," Lori said, shivering. "Hairy, and a mean face!"

"How tall?" Spencer asked.

"Maybe nine or ten feet," Lori said. "Please, can we go find Leo?"

"It sure has big feet," Justin said.

They turned and saw Justin measuring his sneaker next to the imprint in the mud. The print showed a clawed foot with six toes.

"We're lucky it rained earlier. We can follow the tracks!" Spencer exclaimed.

"I see more footprints that way," Justin said, pointing across the field.

They followed the tracks into a forest until they stopped.

Spencer put a finger to his mouth to tell everyone to keep quiet. The three of them looked around, trying to spot the creature.

Then they heard rustling in a nearby tree. They ducked behind a group of bushes. Lori peeked over the top in the direction of the noise.

"Do you see anything?" Spencer whispered.

"No, but I hear something in the trees," Lori said. "I'm going to find Leo."

"No," Spencer said, pulling her down by the arm. "I'll go."

"I can't ask you to do that. It's Leo's and my adventure. I don't want the two of you to get hurt."

"It's OUR adventure now," Spencer informed her. "And we're going to help you get him back."

"What should we do?" she asked, tears forming in her eyes.

Spencer looked over the bushes and gasped as he spotted the creature. It was looking up at the huge tree. Its flat face looked like a cross between an ape and a human but with a huge, crooked nose. Drool spilled from its mouth as it studied the tree. Thick hair covered its back, arms, and legs. Its long arms fell to its knees. Spencer shivered as he eyed the large, clawed hands.

"Oh wow, it's scary," Spencer whispered, ducking down.

Lori popped her head up to look. "I don't see Leo!" she said in a weak voice. "What if he's hurt?" She started shaking and struggled to catch her breath.

"You have to stay calm, Lori," Spencer said. "We need to think." That gave him an idea. He reached into his pocket, pulled out the clear crystal and handed it to her. "Here, take this."

"Why are you giving me this?" she asked, breathing fast.

"Just hold onto it," Spencer instructed, hoping it would help her settle down.

She took it from him and again peeked over the bushes. "I hope it hasn't eaten Leo!"

"I don't think the troll has had enough time to do that," Spencer said.

"And it doesn't have blood all over its face and hands," Justin added.

Lori let out a little yelp at his comment. "Then where is he?" she asked, grasping the crystal in her hand. "I have to go find him!"

"We need to distract the creature so we can see if he's over there," Spencer said.

"How?" she asked.

"Maybe I can get it to chase me," Justin suggested.

"No way!" Spencer exclaimed. "It's bad enough that the monster has Leo . . . " he stopped, looking over to see if his comment further upset Lori.

She stared past him. Spencer followed her gaze and saw that she was studying the wildflowers swaying in the field.

"Valerian root," she said under her breath.

"What about it?" Spencer asked.

She pointed to the light pink and white flowers that stood about three feet high. "My grandmother uses that in her tea at night to relax . . . to help her sleep," she said. "I'll be right back."

Before Spencer could stop her, Lori crept around the bushes and into the field. Spencer remembered that Lori's grandma had taught her about plants.

"Stay here, and keep down," Spencer ordered Justin before following Lori into the field. Her hands and shirt were covered in dirt. She was holding big clumps of flowers that she had pulled out by the roots.

"How are you going to get the troll to eat those?" Spencer asked, figuring out her plan.

"Follow my lead," Lori said. She straightened up and talked loudly. "You can't have this! It's mine! I'm going to eat it all."

The giant troll jerked around to look at them.

"I want it. Give it to me!" Spencer said, acting like he was trying to grab it from her.

"No, this is mine!" Lori shot back, pretending to eat the roots. "Yummy!"

The giant troll suddenly lumbered over, grabbed the clump out of Lori's arms, and shoved the entire plant in its mouth.

Spencer pulled another large clump from the ground. "You can't have this!" he taunted, holding up the clump for the creature to see. The giant ran over and grabbed the plants from Spencer. It pushed him to the ground and then shoved the bundle into its huge mouth. Dirt fell from the sides of its mouth as it chewed with big, crooked teeth.

Spencer and Lori continued teasing the creature and feeding it valerian root until it stopped moving. It patted its belly and loudly burped.

Justin giggled.

The beast turned its head toward the sound. It sniffed the air with its huge nose and started lumbering toward the bushes where Justin was hiding.

"No!" Spencer shouted, waving his arms as he ran after the troll. He got in front and tried to block its path. The giant reached out its long arms to grab him, but Spencer moved out of the way just in time.

Then they heard humming. Spencer recognized it as the sound the bird-bugs made when they flapped their wings. Justin hummed it a little louder.

The troll stopped chasing Spencer and stared at Justin, who was standing up from behind the bushes.

The giant cocked its head, confused by the sound.

Spencer took the opportunity to break away and run toward Justin. He had nearly made it when the creature grabbed the back of his shirt and picked him up. Spencer smelled the creature's breath as it opened its big mouth to take a bite.

CHAPTER
9

Spencer struggled to break free from the giant. But it was no use. The troll was much stronger than him.

"Don't eat him!" Lori shouted, running in front of the troll. She jumped up and down and waved her arms to get its attention. "He tastes awful! Yuck!" she said, bending over and making puking noises. Justin stopped humming and chimed in with Lori.

"He's so gross!" Justin said, pretending to vomit. "He'll make you sick!"

The troll looked at them. It dropped Spencer onto the ground and made puking noises, copying them.

They heard a snicker from up in the tall tree.

"Leo!" Lori shouted, jerking her head toward the tree. "You're alive!"

The giant turned to look at Leo. It growled and ran to the tree.

"Way to blow my hiding spot, Lori!" Leo yelled.

The troll tried to climb the trunk but couldn't get far. It kept sliding back down. Angrily, it grabbed hold of the tree and violently shook it.

"Aaaah!" Leo screamed, slipping from his hiding spot.

"Hang on!" Lori yelled.

The troll shook harder.

Leo lost his grip and started to fall, but then he grabbed onto another branch. His legs swung about three feet above the giant's head.

"Hey, look what I have! Yummy!" Spencer yelled, holding up more valerian root.

The creature ignored Spencer and continued shaking the tree until Leo fell to the ground.

"Leo!" Lori screamed.

"Help me!" Leo cried, kicking at the troll to keep it away.

Spencer picked up a big stick and ran toward the giant. He swung and hit it in the back. The troll growled with anger and swiped its clawed hand at Spencer.

Spencer dodged it and ran around zigzagging with the giant swaying behind him.

"Leo, go over there with Justin," Lori ordered, helping her brother stand up. "Go!"

Leo limped toward the bushes. The troll stopped chasing Spencer and turned its attention to Leo. It ran and grabbed him.

"Help me!" Leo cried, kicking at the creature.

Then the troll opened its mouth wide and roared.

"No!" Lori screamed. "Put him down!"

Justin started humming the bird-bug tune again. The confused beast stopped to listen.

Spencer raised the stick, ready to strike the creature, but Lori held up her hand and shook her head, telling him not to.

The giant troll opened its mouth again. Spencer moved in but stopped when he saw that instead of biting Leo, the creature yawned. It started swaying back and forth to the music.

Justin continued to sing.

Soon, the creature sat down on the ground, still holding Leo in its arms. Finally, it let go of Leo and stretched its arms over its head while loudly yawning.

Leo fled from the creature. He joined Justin in the bushes and started humming the tune with him.

The creature opened its dirty mouth and yawned even longer.

"It's working. He's getting sleepy," Lori said in a low voice, stifling a yawn.

Lori and Spencer stood frozen, watching as the troll's eyes became droopy. The giant fell over and landed with a thud on the ground. Leo and Justin giggled at how loud it snored.

Spencer motioned for the two younger boys to go back across the field. Then he and Lori slowly backed away from the sleeping giant. Once they were sure it wouldn't wake up, they raced to catch up with Justin and Leo.

"Are you okay?" Lori asked her still-limping brother. "Did the creature hurt you?"

"Just scratches and bruises, but I'll be okay," he replied. "Just glad it didn't bite me with those rotten teeth."

"Why were you in the tree?" Justin asked. "Did you climb it to escape?"

"The beast put me there! When it heard you coming, it put me on a limb so I wouldn't get away. While you distracted it, I climbed higher and hid in the leaves so it couldn't see me," Leo explained. "I didn't expect it to shake me out of the tree!"

"I'm so happy you're okay," Lori said, giving him a side hug.

Leo looked embarrassed and wiggled out of her grasp. "I'm fine, I promise."

Lori looked around, and her smile disappeared. "Shoot, I still don't see our door."

"Here's where it should be. I see your markings," Leo said to her. He turned to Justin. "She's always careful to mark where the door was after it disappears."

"Spencer does that, too," Justin said.

"Lori, that was a smart idea to give the troll that root," Spencer said.

"Glad it worked so fast," Lori replied. "It helped that it ate so much, but I think Justin's humming helped as well. Whatever that tune was seemed to calm it down."

"Yah, what was that song?" Leo asked. "Sort of made me sleepy."

"We heard it in the cave, and it stuck in my head," Justin replied. "I was humming it and made Spencer fall asleep. I thought I'd see if it would calm the beast."

"That was a good idea," Spencer said. Then he turned red as Justin told Leo and Lori the story about his falling off the rock and landing in the water.

"Did you guys see the giant spider in the cave?" Justin asked after he finished his story.

"No, we didn't go into a cave," Lori said. "But that sounds terrifying. I don't care for spiders."

"Spencer doesn't either. And it was worse than the monsters," Justin said.

"I was really afraid of the monsters until Lori figured out what made them grow," Leo told them. "She's weird but also really smart."

Spencer smiled, thinking about his "Strange Things Lori Does" list.

"I still don't understand how you know me," Lori said to Spencer, ignoring her brother.

"I saw you in the giant marble. You were on a playground at recess," Spencer responded. In one of his dream-like experiences, he saw young Lori being picked on by two girls. He had also seen her picture as a child at

Ms. Lori's house, but he decided not to tell her that.

"In the marble?" she asked in disbelief.

"Yah," Spencer replied. Seeing how she was looking at him, he wished he hadn't said that. *Now she thinks I'm the strange one.*

"He falls asleep on it all the time," Justin told Leo.

"She does too!" Leo cackled.

Spencer looked at Lori in surprise. "You do? Do you dream when you look at it?"

"Sort of," Lori said, staring at the ground. "It's like I'm awake but somewhere else. And it seems so real until it's over and I realize I'm standing in the same place. I hadn't moved. But I remember everything like it really happened."

"Exactly!" Spencer exclaimed, excited that she understood.

"It hippotizes him," Justin told Leo.

"Here's Lori staring at the marble," Leo said, pressing his head against a large boulder, muttering like a zombie. The two younger boys cracked up.

"I don't know how it happens, but I think what I experience in the marble relates to my life," Lori said, glaring at her brother.

"I agree," Spencer whispered. "Have you heard of a moonstone?"

"Yes, my grandma gave me one last month." She paused, studying Spencer. "Do you think the giant marble is moonstone?"

"They look similar," Spencer replied. "And I read on the internet that a moonstone is known as the *dream stone* in some cultures." Spencer explained what he had learned. He was proud to know more than young Lori since he definitely didn't know more about anything than the older Lori.

"The internet?" Lori asked.

Spencer realized what he had said. He didn't want to explain how far technology had come since she was his age. "I just meant that I read about it," he said.

She nodded. "My grandma gave me a book about crystals for my tenth birthday. She's teaching me about them. She says crystals carry energy." She pulled the clear crystal that he had given her from her pocket. Then she put it back and lowered her voice so only Spencer could hear her. "Do you think it's possible that the bigger the crystal, the more energy it has? That could be why the giant marble is so powerful."

"Yes!" Spencer exclaimed. He had asked Ms. Lori a similar question a few weeks ago. That made him wonder. *Did she know what I was talking about?*

Justin's laugh snapped him out of his thoughts. "Spencer thinks there's a scary woman in the hallway, on the other side of the wall."

"Lori *talks* to that wall! I go over and there's nothing there," Leo said.

Both boys laughed hysterically.

Spencer was annoyed but also intrigued by the look on Lori's face.

"Have you seen her?" Spencer asked.

Lori looked away, not answering him.

CHAPTER
10

"Have you?" Spencer asked again. "Have you seen the woman in black?"

"And Spencer stands forever looking up at the ceiling. He acts like it's a real sky!"

"I think it is real . . . " Lori said in a low voice.

"You do?" Spencer asked, smiling. He loved that young Lori seemed to get him . . .

like the older Lori. "I love how the stars go on forever."

"And how the moons go through the phases," Lori added.

"You guys are so weird," Justin said. "It's a ceiling."

"No doubt," Leo agreed.

Ms. Lori's words circled in Spencer's head. *We're more alike than you know.*

"We'd better keep looking for our door," Lori finally said. "Thank you for helping me get my brother back. I couldn't have done it without you."

"Glad you accepted our help," Spencer said.

Young Lori's face reddened. "Sorry, I'm not used to people helping me . . . or being so nice."

Spencer felt sad. He knew kids were mean to her when she was his age. "They obviously don't see how cool you are."

Lori smiled. "I appreciate that."

"I see the door!" Leo shouted.

Everyone turned to look at the tall, spiky door with blue, green, and purple shapes.

"Oh, thank goodness!" Lori exclaimed.

"That's not like our door at all," Justin noted.

"We'd better go through it before it disappears," Lori said.

"It was good to meet you. I didn't think anyone was as weird as my sister until I met your brother!" Leo said, making Justin crack up.

Spencer smacked his brother on the arm as they watched Lori and Leo walk through the opening.

"Goodbye! Glad we met you, and thank you again for your help," Lori said, smiling.

Leo waved. "Maybe we'll see you back in Colorado, or on another adventure!"

Spencer and Justin waved back and watched the door close and disappear.

"I like Leo. I'm sad to see them go," Justin said.

"Me too," Spencer said, staring at where the door had been. He wished he had asked young Lori more about the figure in the wall. Finally, he turned around. "We'd better find our door and get home."

They could hear the little creatures chirping and growling as they jogged down the path to their door.

"They aren't so scary now," Justin said, giggling at the colorful heads popping up over the tall grasses.

Just then, a teal creature with white legs and four big eyes darted out of the grasses and nipped at Justin's heel.

"What was that?" Justin shouted in surprise as he turned to look at the creature. It growled at him while wagging its three tails. "Oh, I'm so going to get you for that!" he said, chasing the little monster back into the field. Several other creatures raced after Justin, loudly chirping. Suddenly, Justin tripped over a yellow monster with orange triangles and fell to the ground.

In an instant, several little creatures jumped on top of him. Justin started to panic.

They started to grow! He was about to scream for help when he remembered what Lori had said. Justin forced himself to giggle. The creatures shrank again, and a furry red one jumped on his chest and started licking his face. Justin laughed and tried to wiggle away from it.

"Justin!" Spencer yelled. "Will you stop messing around? I want to get back!"

"Okay little fellows, I have to go. Mr. Grumpy over there is in a hurry," Justin said, moving the creatures off his stomach so he could stand up.

"I'm not grumpy. I just want to talk to Ms. Lori," Spencer replied.

Justin continued to remove the little monsters that clung to his legs as he returned to the path. After the last creature was off him, he jogged to catch up with Spencer.

Finally, they were back at the group of large boulders. They searched for a while until they found the line of grapefruit-sized rocks and the arrow made from sticks.

"This has to be the right one," Spencer said, looking at the green and blue wildflowers on the hill above the rock.

"But it doesn't have the orange circles on it," Justin pointed out. "How are we going to open it?"

"Don't know," Spencer muttered, distracted. "I still can't believe we ran into Lori and Leo, and they went on adventures like us."

"Funny seeing Lori at your age," Justin replied, laughing. "She's as weird as you!"

"Lori isn't weird," Spencer said defensively. "Just shy. And really smart. She figured out what made the monsters grow. They would have eaten us if she hadn't come along. And she got the creepy troll to eat the roots and fall asleep. That was really smart."

Spencer realized he had been calling Lori strange all summer and now he was defending her.

"Well, I made it sleepy by humming that song to it," Justin responded. "That makes me smart, too."

Spencer nodded. He was thinking about how many times over the summer Ms. Lori had told him how much they had in common. He thought about how hard he had been on her at the beginning of the summer. Now he knew that at his age she had also struggled with issues of self-doubt and lack of confidence. *Maybe that's why she understands me so well,* he thought.

"The circles are back!" Justin exclaimed as the door suddenly lit up. "Here's the circle we touched last time."

They placed their hands on the orange spot toward the bottom, making the circles flash. The huge rock rolled forward.

Once they were in the circular room, the big boulder rolled back to the wall and disappeared. Soon, a new door filled the empty spot on the wall.

"Ms. Lori has to remember meeting us, right?" Justin asked. "Do you think she knows we go on adventures while she watches TV?"

"That's my first question when we get back," Spencer replied. He looked at the domed sky ceiling. All summer, he had wished he could tell Lori about the amazing room since he knew she loved space. Now he knew she had seen it. *And she also thought it was a real sky!* As much as he wanted to stay in that magical room forever, he couldn't wait to talk to his nanny.

They headed to the black hallway door and placed their hands on the metal handle.

"I hope this isn't the last time we're here," Spencer whispered, turning to gaze again at the amazing circular room.

As they walked down the hall toward the slide, Spencer watched the wall to his right. He remembered what Leo had said about Lori talking to the wall. *Has she seen the woman?*

Suddenly, there she was. The woman in black was in the mirrored wall right in front of him! She was wearing the black cloak, and the hood was down so he could see her long white hair.

"Remember when we tried so hard to run up this slide and couldn't?" Justin asked. "I was the one who sat down on the edge and figured it out. You know, you say I can't read but I'm really smart. I figured out a lot of things on our adventures," Justin said, chattering away. "Are you listening to me?"

"She's here . . . and she's real," Spencer whispered, staring into the woman's piercing green eyes that glowed in the flickering light. He couldn't believe he was actually happy to see her. He smiled.

"Didn't you want to get back to talk to Ms. Lori?" Justin asked.

The woman smiled back which made her look younger. She looked like the teacher from his dream in the marble. He was fairly certain the same woman had been with him in several of his marble experiences. He had written about them in his journal. At first, he had thought she was trying to scare or harm him. Now he knew she had been trying to help.

"Thank you," Spencer said to the woman in the wall.

She nodded and smiled.

"Spencer!" Justin shouted. "I asked if I should go!"

"Sorry, yes, go ahead," he said, moving to the slide. "See you up there."

Justin sat on the edge. Suddenly, his hair and shirt stood up as he was pulled backward up the slide.

"Woo-hoo!" Justin yelled, disappearing beyond the second curve.

Spencer glanced back at the woman on the other side of the wall. He smiled and waved to her. She lifted her arm in the black cloak and waved.

"Hopefully, this isn't goodbye forever," Spencer whispered.

He sat down on the edge of the slide. A strong tug pulled him up and around the curves until he was at the top. Spencer felt the familiar push and slid back under the couch in his living room. He crawled out to find his brother waiting for him.

CHAPTER
11

"What are you going to say to Ms. Lori?" Justin asked.

"I'm not sure," Spencer replied, brushing the dust off his now-dry shirt. Butterflies danced in his stomach as he walked into the family room to confront her.

Lori glanced up from the TV. She sat up in her chair when she saw Spencer's face.

"You okay?" she asked, muting the TV with the remote.

"You . . . you knew, didn't you?" Spencer stammered.

"I knew what?" she asked, staring at him through her thick glasses.

"About the couch," he said. "About all of it."

"Ah," she said, smiling. "I wondered when this day would come."

"You knew about our adventures?" Justin asked, trying to keep up.

"Yes," Lori admitted.

"Why didn't you say anything?" Spencer asked. "Why didn't you tell us that you went on adventures?"

"I wasn't supposed to. The experiences were for you. And I knew at some point we would meet on one of your adventures, and when we did, we would have this discussion," she said.

"So, we both have magical couches?" Justin asked.

Lori looked at Spencer and smiled. "There is only one couch."

"I knew it!" Spencer said. "So you knew that my dad bought your grandma's couch?"

"Not at first," Lori said. "After meeting you on the adventure over thirty years ago, I thought there were two couches. Or more. But eventually, I knew there was only one."

"How?" Spencer asked, sitting on the arm of a chair, looking intensely at Lori.

"First, two boys around my age said I was their nanny. I couldn't understand it at the time," she said.

Spencer nodded. He couldn't imagine how strange that must have been to hear.

"I thought about our meeting so many times and what it all meant. I came up with different scenarios. But my grandma's couch was special . . . magical. I just knew there was only one couch."

"But your couch was red," Justin said.

"My Grandma Laurel replaced the red fabric a few years ago," Lori said. "To cream."

"Really?" Justin asked, his eyes growing big. "But why did you get rid of the couch? I'd want to keep it forever."

"My dad didn't know how special it was to me when he sold it to the antique store. I had planned to help him clean out my grandmother's place after she passed. I already had a trip planned with friends. He thought he was helping by doing most of the work while I was gone. The couch was old, and he didn't think anyone would want it. When I found out, I called the store, but the saleslady told me someone had already bought it."

"My dad," Spencer said softly.

"I was devastated," Lori said.

"Did the lady tell you we had it?" Justin asked.

"She wouldn't give me your information. I was thinking about putting an ad on the internet to find it. That was about the time a friend told me that a family had just moved into town and was looking for help over the summer watching their two boys.

When I talked to your mother and heard your names, I wondered if it could be you. I didn't know for sure until I saw the couch in your living room."

"Did you take the job just to find the couch?" Spencer asked, not sure he wanted to hear her answer.

Lori smiled. "Actually, I took it because I was meant to be your nanny."

"Are you going to take your couch back?" Justin asked.

Lori thought for a moment. "I love that couch, but I believe it's exactly where it's supposed to be. You two were meant to go on adventures together and learn valuable lessons, just like Leo and me."

"I like Leo," Justin said. "He's funny!"

"I remember how well the two of you got along. He liked you as well. You remind me of him in many ways."

"Same bad jokes," Spencer said.

Lori chuckled.

"Leo and I laughed so hard about the two of you being weird," Justin said, giggling.

"Oh, I remember," Lori said, smiling.

Spencer stared at his nanny, thinking about how much he had in common with her even though she was his mother's age. *More than I ever knew.*

"Why did you stop going on adventures?" Justin asked.

She sighed. "We had been going for a long time. Then one day, we couldn't get through. I didn't understand why and was so upset. Leo finally told me the truth. He had told his best friend about it," Lori said, looking sad. "They tried to go without me. Of course, it didn't work, and his friend thought he was crazy. I kept telling him we couldn't discuss it except with each other. I knew it was a rule of the couch."

"See, Justin? I told you we couldn't tell anyone!" Spencer said.

"I know! I haven't!" Justin retorted.

"He almost slipped up with our parents several times," Spencer said. "I knew we had to keep it a secret."

"You were right," Lori said. "After that, we never got through to the under-the-couch world again."

"Why do you think *we* got the couch?" Spencer asked.

"All I know is that Leo and I grew much closer because of the adventures. We learned so much, and the experiences helped me to understand and accept myself." She looked directly into Spencer's eyes.

"Self-love," he whispered, understanding what she meant. He knew that between Lori and the couch adventures, he had gained a lot of confidence over the summer.

"The under-the-couch world helps you not only live your dreams but face your fears and find your strengths," she said. "You learn valuable lessons through the experiences."

"Spencer learned about spiders, which he is still scared of!" Justin said. "On one adventure, he . . . "

Lori raised her hand. "Another unwritten rule of the couch is that you only share the experiences with the person who was on the adventure with you."

"I still don't understand why the couch is so special," Spencer said. "You said it was your grandma's?"

"Yes, but originally, it was her grandmother's. Luyu's husband made it for her from a huge old tree that was on the land where she grew up. She loved that tree. But one day, there was a terrible storm they called 'the storm of the century.' Lightning struck it and split it in two. Luyu was heartbroken. Her husband was a good carpenter and made the couch from the wood of that tree."

"So that's why it's magical — because of the lightning?" Justin asked.

"Perhaps," Lori replied.

Justin looked confused. "Did your grandma know about the couch . . . and the under-the-couch world?"

"I don't know," Lori answered. "I never talked to her about it."

"So you knew all summer we were going on adventures," Spencer said again.

"Yes," she admitted. "I was so happy you discovered the secrets of the couch."

"And you knew I was talking about the marble in the circular room when I asked you about the moonstone?" Spencer inquired.

Lori nodded. "You're the one who originally made me realize it was a moonstone."

Spencer looked at her strangely. Then he remembered their discussion and how he had slipped and mentioned the internet. "Your grandma gave you one," Spencer recalled.

"Yes, which reminds me . . . " Lori got out of the chair and grabbed her large shoulder bag. She dug through it and pulled out a clear, rectangular object.

"You kept it?" Spencer asked.

"All these years," Lori replied.

"What kind of crystal is it?" Spencer asked.

"Selenite," she responded. "Liquid light. It's a high vibrational stone of calmness, insight, and profound wisdom."

Justin looked confused, so Spencer explained, "I gave it to young Lori to help her settle down and think more clearly after the troll took Leo."

"And it worked," Lori said. "Justin, you asked me a few weeks ago at my house which crystal was my favorite. This one is . . . because a boy my age was so kind to me when many weren't."

Spencer blushed at the compliment. "And you accepted our help!"

Lori smiled. "You know, your kindness had a huge effect on me. I never forgot that. People don't realize how much they impact others with their words and actions."

CHAPTER
12

Spencer stared at Lori and thought about her words.

"Leo and I thought it was funny how you both fell asleep on the marble and stared at the ceiling and talked to the hallway wall," Justin said.

"Oh yah!" Spencer exclaimed. "Ms. Lori, did you see the woman in black on the other side of the wall?"

Lori turned to stare at the TV in the family room, even though the sound was off.

"I asked you when we were on the adventure, but you never answered me. You saw her, didn't you?" Spencer pressed.

Finally, Lori nodded.

"See, Justin? Ms. Lori saw her!"

"Leo and I didn't," Justin said.

"You saw the old woman with the black cloak, the long white hair, and the green piercing eyes?" Spencer asked, wanting to make sure they were talking about the same person.

"Yes," Lori replied, studying him with her big brown eyes.

"I knew it!" Spencer said, punching the air. "I knew from your response, as young Lori, that you saw her!"

"Spencer was super scared of her," Justin said. "He would scream and fall down in the hallway when he saw her."

Spencer glared at his brother.

"Did she do something to frighten you?" Lori asked.

Spencer hesitated as he thought about it. "No. Just seeing her was scary. But, as I learned today — from you, actually — fear makes things bigger than they are."

"Good lesson," Lori said. "You can't give your power away to fear."

"Why is the woman in the under-the-couch world?" Spencer asked. "I saw her in the wall, and she was in a lot of my experiences in the marble. Was she in your dreams, too?"

"Yes," Lori answered. "You know who she is, don't you?"

"No," Spencer answered, shocked by her response. "Who?"

"Do you remember me telling you that only two percent of the population has green eyes?" Lori asked.

"You said that at your house. You wanted green eyes like your grandma, but I said I liked your brown eyes," Justin said, smiling sweetly.

Spencer stared at her with his mouth open. "Laurel?"

"No, although she also had green eyes," Lori replied.

Spencer furrowed his brow, recalling the conversation at Lori's house. Then it hit him! He knew who the woman in the black cloak was! The picture at Lori's house was in black and white, but Lori had mentioned her green eyes.

"Luyu, your great-great grandmother!"

"I don't get it," Justin said. "Isn't she dead? How could you see her in the hallway?"

"It was her couch," Spencer whispered.

"But why was she in the wall?" he asked. "Was she magical or something?"

"I thought she was," Lori responded.

"But why could the two of us see her, but not Justin or Leo?"

"I told you that we were alike in many ways," she said, repeating what she had said many times before. "She helped you, yes?"

"Yah, she did," Spencer replied, sitting back down. "But I don't get what you're saying."

Lori smiled but didn't explain.

Spencer wished Lori could have stayed all night. He could have talked to her forever.

Of course, his mother came home from work early, which rarely happened. When Lori left, she let him know that they could continue their discussion the next day. Spencer was happy that he had a few more days with her before he went back to school.

While his mom started dinner and Justin played with his Legos, Spencer grabbed the laptop and ran upstairs to his room. He took his journal out of his nightstand and flipped the pages to start a fourth section. He wrote down all the questions that were swirling in his head. He had so much he still wanted to ask Lori about Luyu and the under-the-couch world.

He glanced at the first section of his journal. He smiled at his list of "Strange Things Lori Does." Lori didn't seem so strange and mysterious to him anymore, not like at the beginning of the summer. But now he knew her secret . . . and it wasn't at all what he had expected.

Then Spencer turned to the second section of his journal and wrote about his dream while gazing into the giant blue marble. He remembered how panicked he felt standing at the front of the classroom, struggling to talk. Words wouldn't come out of his mouth until the feathers fell from the ceiling.

He looked up the meaning of a blue feather and learned it was associated with finding the truth and letting go of anything that's holding you back. He read that blue was the color of the throat chakra. Lori had taught them about the seven chakras and told them they were energy centers. He read that the throat chakra is the center of speaking one's truth and about accepting oneself.

Spencer glanced through his journal. He had written about several experiences that taught him lessons around acceptance and self-love. He now knew that young Lori struggled with the same issues.

"Lori and Luyu were helping me all summer," he whispered.

"What are you doing?" Justin asked, barging into his room.

Spencer jumped. "What does it look like I'm doing?"

"Writing about everything that happened today?" Justin asked, plopping himself on the end of the bed. "Did you write about running into Lori and Leo?" he asked. "And about how the troll took Leo?"

"Not yet," Spencer replied, flipping to the third section of his journal about their adventures. He quickly jotted down notes.

"And about the bats, the huge spider, and the glowing bird-bugs that made that humming sound? And how smart I was humming it and making the troll fall asleep?"

"Okay, slow down," Spencer said, writing as fast as he could.

"And about that room with all the crystals that made us feel good," Justin added.

"Selenite," Spencer said, smiling at how Lori had kept it all these years.

"And don't forget how Lori saved us. She told us that fear made the monsters grow."

Spencer wrote the word "fear." As he

stared at the word, he recalled what Lori had said about not giving your power away to fear. He thought about how afraid he had been about a lot of things that summer, especially about making new friends and starting a new school.

"But not anymore."

"Not anymore . . . what?" Justin asked.

I'm not afraid anymore, Spencer thought to himself.

"Dinner!" called their mother from the bottom of the stairs.

"Oh, right," Justin said, jumping off the bed. "I came up here cuz I was supposed to tell you to come set the table."

"Tell Mom I'll be right there," Spencer said. He added "no more" in front of the word "fear" and then shoved the journal under the junk in his nightstand drawer.

He smiled as he headed down the stairs to the kitchen, thinking about Lori and Leo going on adventures. He knew the experiences of going under the couch had changed him.

He had learned so much over the summer, both from the adventures and from Lori.

He couldn't wait to see his nanny the next day and was already looking forward to when she could come back and stay with them during the school year.

SUSAN LINTONSMITH is a business executive and author who went from climbing the corporate ladder to falling under the couch.

Susan lives in Colorado where she enjoys the mountains and outdoors. When not working, she loves writing, hiking, cooking, and spending time with family, friends, and her two dogs.

She has published twelve books in the Under the Couch series: *Hide and Seek*, *Rainbow*, *Spiders*, *Colors*, *Flipped*, *Video Games*, *Candy*, *Mother Nature*, *Castle*, *Crystals*, *Spaceship*, and *Creatures*. The books progress over the summer as two brothers go on fun yet dangerous adventures and learn valuable lessons through their experiences.

Her goal is that all kids, especially those who struggle with reading like her sons, will enjoy the adventures Spencer and Justin go on in the Under the Couch series.

Visit her website at underthecouchbooks.com

READ THE UNDER THE COUCH SERIES IN ORDER,
STARTING WITH BOOK 1, HIDE AND SEEK,
AND DISCOVER THE SECRETS OF THE COUCH!

Book 1, *Hide and Seek*, book 2, *Rainbow*,
book 3, *Spiders*, book 4, *Colors*, book 5, *Flipped*,
book 6, *Video Games*, book 7, *Candy*,
book 8, *Mother Nature*, book 9, *Castle*,
book 10, *Crystals*, book 11, *Spaceship*, and
book 12, *Creatures*.

UNDER THE COUCH
BOOK 4
Colors
SUSAN LINTONSMITH

UNDER THE COUCH
BOOK 5
Flipped
SUSAN LINTONSMITH

UNDER THE COUCH
BOOK 6
Video Games
SUSAN LINTONSMITH

UNDER THE COUCH
BOOK 7
Candy
SUSAN LINTONSMITH

UNDER THE COUCH
BOOK 8
Mother Nature
SUSAN LINTONSMITH

UNDER THE COUCH
BOOK 9
Castle
SUSAN LINTONSMITH

UNDER THE COUCH
BOOK 10
Crystals
SUSAN LINTONSMITH

UNDER THE COUCH
BOOK 11
Spaceship
SUSAN LINTONSMITH

UNDER THE COUCH
BOOK 12
Creatures
SUSAN LINTONSMITH

9 781736 891117